The Countries
Czech Republic

Kristin Van Cleaf
ABDO Publishing Company

visit us at
www.abdopublishing.com

Published by ABDO Publishing Company, 8000 West 78th Street, Edina, Minnesota 55439. Copyright © 2008 by Abdo Consulting Group, Inc. International copyrights reserved in all countries. No part of this book may be reproduced in any form without written permission from the publisher. The Checkerboard Library™ is a trademark and logo of ABDO Publishing Company.

Printed in the United States.

Interior Photos: Alamy pp. 4, 6, 19, 22, 25, 26, 27, 28, 29, 31, 33, 35, 36, 37; Corbis pp. 9, 11, 12, 14, 21; Getty Images p. 13; Peter Arnold pp. 5, 18

Editors: Rochelle Baltzer, Heidi M.D. Elston
Art Direction & Maps: Neil Klinepier

Library of Congress Cataloging-in-Publication Data

Van Cleaf, Kristin, 1976-
 Czech Republic / Kristin Van Cleaf.
      p. cm. -- (The countries)
 Includes index.
 ISBN 978-1-59928-782-9
 1. Czech Republic--Juvenile literature. I. Title.

DB2011.V36 2007
943.71--dc22

2007010179

Contents

Dobrý Den! 4
Fast Facts 6
Timeline 7
Past to Present 8
Heart of Europe 14
Nature 18
Czechs 20
Free Market 24
Historic Sites 26
Travel and News 28
Parliament Rules 30
Let's Celebrate! 32
Rich Culture 34
Glossary 38
Web Sites 39
Index 40

Dobrý Den!

The Czech Republic is a great location for an active vacation.

Hello from the Czech Republic! This small central European country boasts a varied landscape of hills, mountains, and lowlands. And, people from all over the world visit its limestone caves.

The Czech Republic is split into two regions. Moravia covers the eastern part of the country, while Bohemia is in the west. Prague (PRAHG), the republic's capital, is located in Bohemia. The city is thought to be one of the most beautiful in Europe.

Most of the republic's people are Czech. Czechs are a Slavic people with close ties to the people of neighboring Slovakia. At different times in history, the Czech and Slovak republics were one country called Czechoslovakia. Then in

Dobrý Den!

Dobrý den *from the Czech Republic!*

1993, Czechoslovakia split into the Czech Republic and Slovakia.

The Czechs have established and preserved their own **culture** through many centuries. They have experienced hardships. But today, the Czechs continue to strengthen their country.

Fast Facts

OFFICIAL NAME: Czech Republic
CAPITAL: Prague

LAND
- Area: 30,450 square miles (78,866 sq km)
- Mountain Range: Bohemian-Moravian Highlands
- Highest Point: Sněžka 5,256 feet (1,602 m)
- Major Rivers: Elbe, Vltava, Oder

PEOPLE
- Population: 10,228,744 (July 2007 estimate)
- Major Cities: Prague, Brno, Ostrava, Plzeň
- Official Language: Czech
- Religions: Roman Catholicism, Protestantism

GOVERNMENT
- Form: Parliamentary democracy
- Head of State: President
- Head of Government: Prime minister
- Legislature: Bicameral parliament
- Nationhood: January 1, 1993

ECONOMY
- Agricultural Products: Wheat, potatoes, sugar beets, hops, fruit, pigs, poultry
- Mining Products: Coal
- Manufactured Products: Machinery and equipment, motor vehicles, glass, metal, weapons
- Money: Czech koruna (1 koruna = 100 haleru)

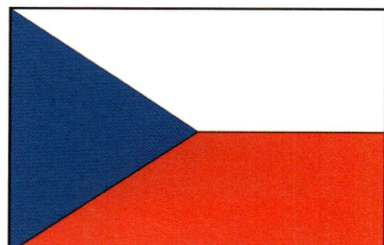

Czech Republic's flag

Czech koruny

Timeline

400s BC	Present-day Czech Republic is first occupied by Celtic peoples
AD 800s	The Great Moravian Empire is created
1346	Charles IV becomes king of Bohemia
1526	Bohemia and Moravia fall under the control of the Austrian Habsburg family
1618	Czechs revolt against Habsburg control
1700s	Czech culture and language is slowly brought back to the country
1918	Czechoslovakia is formed on October 28
1939	On March 15, Germany invades Czechoslovakia
1940s	Communism gains support in Czechoslovakia
1989	In November, the Velvet Revolution occurs; the communist government steps down
1990	The people of Czechoslovakia elect a democratic government
1993	On January 1, Czechoslovakia splits into two independent countries, Slovakia and the Czech Republic
1999	The Czech Republic joins NATO
2004	The Czech Republic joins the European Union

Past to Present

The Czech Republic is a fairly new country. It was founded on January 1, 1993, when Czechoslovakia split into the Czech Republic and Slovakia. Even though the Czech Republic is a young country, its history is rich.

Celtic peoples were likely living in today's Czech Republic as early as the 400s BC. Gradually, **Germanic** tribes moved to the area. By about AD 500, Slavic peoples had also settled there.

In the 800s, various Slavic tribes banded together and created their own state. It became known as the Great Moravian Empire. This empire grew to include Bohemia, southern Poland, Slovakia, and western Hungary. But by 907, Hungarian tribes had conquered Great Moravia.

Over the next 400 years, Bohemia rose to greatness. In the 1200s, many Germans moved into western and northern Bohemia. Their skills in farming, mining, crafting, and other areas enriched the Czech **culture**.

Today, a Jan Hus monument dominates Old Town Square in Prague. This memorial stands as a symbol of the fight for Czech independence.

In 1346, Charles IV became king of Bohemia. His reign is thought of as a golden age for the area. King Charles turned Prague into one of Europe's main **cultural** centers.

In the late 1300s, preacher Jan Hus led a movement to reform the Roman Catholic Church. Hus's death in 1415 sparked a series of religious wars that lasted until 1436. After this, **Protestantism** spread.

In 1526, the Austrian Habsburg family took control of Bohemia and Moravia. The Habsburgs were Roman Catholics. This caused conflict with the Czech **Protestants**. They revolted in 1618, which began the Thirty Years' War. This series of wars occurred throughout Europe.

Under Habsburg rule, Czech **culture** began to disappear. The Habsburgs forced the Czech people to convert to Catholicism and speak German. German ways of life spread throughout the region.

In the late 1700s, scholars and nobles began restoring Czech culture and language. They succeeded in re-creating a national identity. By the mid-1800s, the people were pushing for self-government. However, Austria continued to rule Bohemia and Moravia into the 1900s.

When **World War I** broke out, leaders such as Tomáš Masaryk tried to gain international support for independence. The effort was successful. On October 28, 1918, Czechoslovakia was formed. Masaryk served as the country's first president until 1935.

The country prospered for a time. Then in 1938, German **dictator** Adolf Hitler demanded that Czechoslovakia hand

Past to Present 11

over the Sudetenland (soo-DAYT-uhn-land), Czechoslovakia's western border regions. Hoping to avoid war, European rulers signed the Munich Agreement. This gave the Sudetenland to Germany.

On March 15, 1939, Germany invaded Czechoslovakia during **World War II**. The people of Bohemia and Moravia

Edvard Beneš (right) helped Tomáš Masaryk (left) found Czechoslovakia. Beneš later became the nation's second president.

resisted throughout the German occupation. About 250,000 Czechs died during the war.

When **World War II** ended, Czechoslovakia's exiled government returned. However, **communism** quickly gained support in Czechoslovakia in the late 1940s. By 1948, communist leaders controlled the government. However after the first few years, the new government lost much of its popular support.

Czechoslovakia's **economy** weakened in the 1960s. **Rebellion** broke out, but it was quickly suppressed. Still, dissatisfaction continued among the people.

During the Velvet Revolution, crowds of Czechs protested communism in Czechoslovakia.

Throughout the 1980s, the standard of living in Czechoslovakia fell. And, support for the communist government also lessened. Demonstrations in November 1989 eventually led to the communist government stepping down. This is known today as the Velvet Revolution, because it occurred peacefully.

In 1990, the people elected a **democratic** government. However, many Slovaks were unhappy. So on January 1, 1993, Czechoslovakia was replaced by the Czech Republic and Slovakia.

Czechs proudly hold the European Union flag.

The Czech Republic built itself as a **parliamentary democracy**. It put a **free market** in place. In 1999, it joined **NATO**. And, the Czech Republic joined the **European Union** in 2004.

Heart of Europe

The Czech Republic is located in the center of Europe. Germany borders it to the west. Austria lies south, and Slovakia is to the east. And, Poland shares the republic's northern border.

The Czech Republic is a land of grand beauty. The western region, Bohemia, is a **plateau** ringed by mountains and hills. The Bohemian Forest lies in the southwest of this area.

The Ore Mountains are in northwestern Bohemia. As their name suggests, they contain many mineral metals. The Ore Mountains top out at about 2,800 feet (850 m). The Sudety Mountains lie in the northeast. There, the country's highest point at 5,256 feet (1,602 m) is Sněžka (SNYEHSH-kuh).

Plains and plateaus make up the center of Bohemia. Rich farming soil is abundant in the northern section. Farther south, the rocky land contains coal and many minerals such as iron and silver ore.

Bohemian Forest

Germany
Poland
CZECH REPUBLIC
Austria
Slovakia

North America
Europe
Asia
DETAIL AREA
Africa
South America
Australia
Antarctica

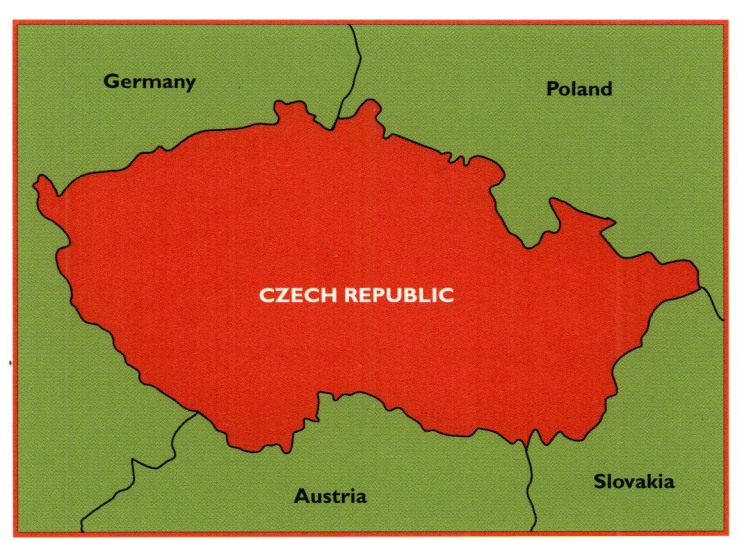

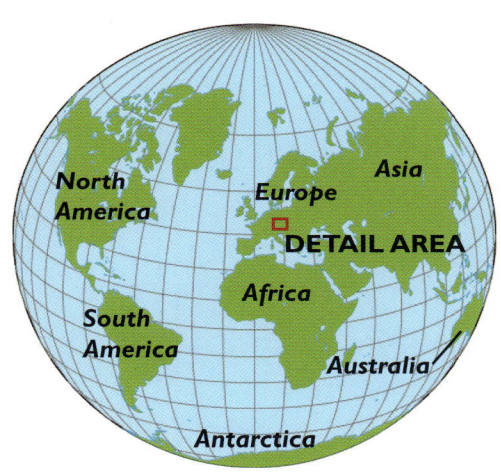

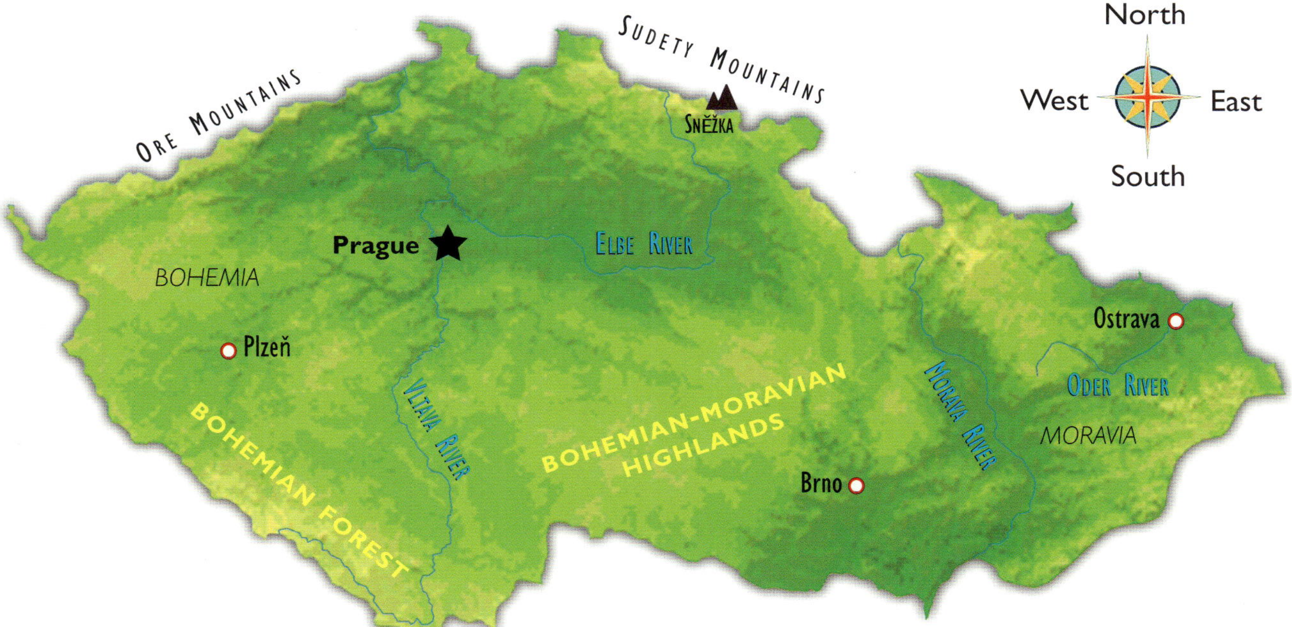
Sudety Mountains
Ore Mountains
Sněžka
North
West
East
South
Prague
Elbe River
Bohemia
Plzeň
Ostrava
Oder River
Vltava River
Morava River
Bohemian-Moravian Highlands
Moravia
Bohemian Forest
Brno

South of the Bohemian **plateau** are the Bohemian-Moravian Highlands. This region is made up of low hills, plateaus, and high plains. It also includes the Moravian Karst. This cluster of limestone caves contains many underground passages and lakes.

Southeast of Bohemia are the Moravian lowlands. Rich soil makes the region good for farming. A wide pass called the Moravian Gate separates the Sudety Mountains from the Carpathian Mountains of Slovakia.

The Elbe River flows across Bohemia to the southwest. Along its course, the Vltava (VUHL-tuh-vuh), Ohře (AWR-zheh), and Jizera rivers join it as it drains into Germany. In the east, the Morava River moves southward, eventually reaching the Danube River. The Oder River lies in the northeast and flows into Poland. Many mineral springs are also found throughout the country.

The Czech Republic's climate changes by region and elevation. Summers are warm in the mountains and hot in the lowlands. July is the wettest month, while February is the driest. Winters are chilly overall, but coldest in the mountains. And, winters may bring snow. However, the highest peaks have snow year-round.

Heart of Europe 17

Rainfall

AVERAGE YEARLY RAINFALL

Inches		Centimeters
Under 20		Under 50
20–40		50–100
40–60		100–150
Over 60		Over 150

Temperature

AVERAGE TEMPERATURE

Fahrenheit		Celsius
Over 76°		Over 24°
65°–76°		18°–24°
54°–65°		12°–18°
32°–54°		0°–12°
21°–32°		-6°–0°
Below 21°		Below -6°

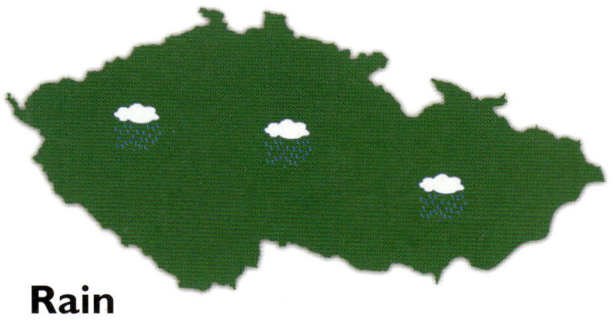

Rain

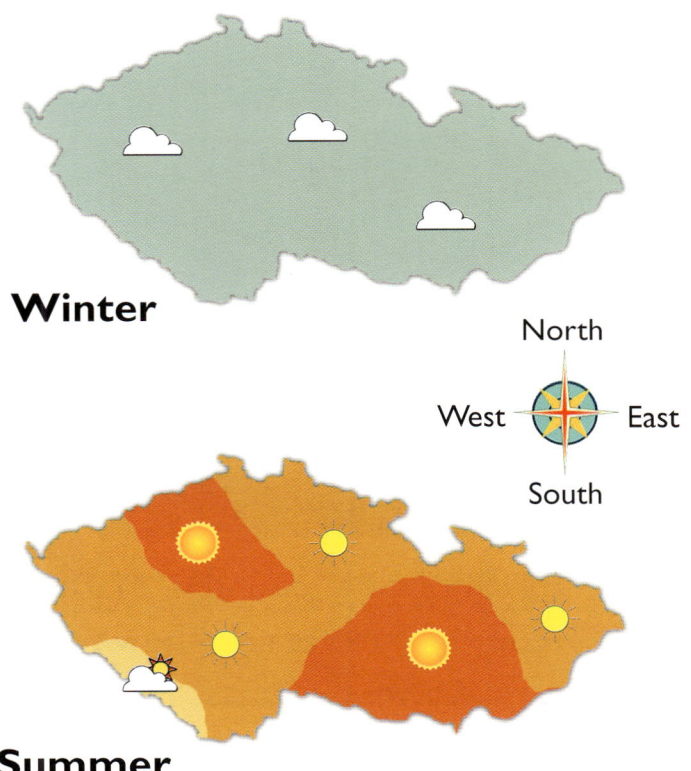

Winter

Summer

Nature

Much of the Czech Republic's forests have been cut for timber and farmland. But many trees still flourish. Oak, beech, and spruce trees are most common.

The tree line is at about 4,500 feet (1,370 m) above sea level. Past this point, trees cannot grow. There, you will find only grasses and shrubs. Below this line, fir, spruce, and dwarf pines are common.

Mouflon

Many types of animals live in the Czech Republic. Common birds are ducks, partridges, pheasants, and wild geese. Rarer birds, such as vultures, eagles, ospreys, eagle owls, and capercaillie, are protected.

Small animals are found throughout the country. Marmots, otters, martens, and minks live in the forests and the wetlands. Larger animals include bears, wolves, wildcats, and lynx.

The government works to protect the country's wildlife and landscape. Animal species in danger of becoming extinct are raised in special game reserves. This is true for the mouflon mountain sheep.

The government has also set aside areas of land as nature reserves to preserve the landscape. These include the Šumava Forest, the Jizera Mountains, and the Moravian Karst.

Šumava National Park and Protected Landscape Area

Czechs

About 90 percent of Czech Republic citizens are Czech. Nearly 4 percent are Moravian, while 2 percent are Slovak. German, Hungarian, Polish, and Roma people also live there.

Before **World War II**, Czechoslovakia had many Jewish citizens. Sadly, many were killed during the war. Today, between 5,000 and 10,000 Jews live in the Czech Republic. Prague boasts a large Jewish community.

The country's official language is Czech. However, Moravians have their own **dialect**. Also, some people speak Slovak, which is related to Czech. Other people speak their **culture**'s language.

Most rural citizens live in single-family houses. They commonly work on farms. But, some people commute to the cities for work. In cities, Czechs often live in apartments.

Today, the cities are experiencing a housing shortage. And, much of the available housing is poor quality from **communist** times. Many cities suffer from air pollution and some crime. Even so, the Czech Republic has one of the highest living standards of the formerly communist Eastern European countries.

Housing in the Czech Republic

Since the fall of **communism** in the Czech Republic, religious freedom is again allowed. Today, about 27 percent of Czechs are Roman Catholic. A small number are **Protestant**. Still, many embrace no religion.

Education is important to Czechs. Children may begin kindergarten at age three. All children must attend school from ages 6 to 16. They often learn a foreign language. Students have the option of continuing their education at a technical or general education school. Some may pursue teacher training.

Some of the best universities in the Czech Republic have been around for hundreds of years. Two located in Prague are among the oldest in central Europe. Charles University was founded in 1348. And, the Czech Technical University opened in 1707.

Czechs enjoy rich foods. Pork and boiled dumplings are two favorites. Pickled cabbage is well liked, too. Carp and potato salad are often eaten at Christmas. And, apple strudel is a popular dessert.

Czech food is filling!

Potato Dumplings

Czechs enjoy potato dumplings with meat and sauce.

- 6 medium potatoes, peeled
- 1 1/2 teaspoons salt
- 1 egg
- 1 1/2 to 2 cups gravy thickener

Boil potatoes in a small amount of water until tender. Drain potatoes. Then mash them and let them cool. On a floured board, slowly add gravy thickener to the potatoes, working the mixture into a dough with your hands. Add egg and salt. Shape the potato mixture into a long roll and cut into ten slices. Drop dumplings into boiling water. Boil gently for about five minutes, or until the dumplings float to the top. Drain the dumplings on a paper towel.

AN IMPORTANT NOTE TO THE CHEF: Always have an adult help with the preparation and cooking of food. Never use kitchen utensils or appliances without adult permission and supervision.

LANGUAGE

English	Czech
Hello	Dobrý den (DOH-bree dehn)
Yes	Ano (AH-noh)
No	Ne (neh)
Please	Prosím (PROH-zeem)
Thank you	Děkuji (DYACK-quee)
Good-bye	Na shledanou (nah SKLEH-dah-now)

Free Market

During the Czech Republic's **communist** years, the government managed all parts of the **economy**. After the change in government, the economy quickly became a **free market**.

Coal, lignite, and uranium are the country's main resources. Russia, Austria, Germany, Hungary, and Slovakia are a few of the Czech Republic's trading partners. Czechs export coal, automobiles, footwear, iron, steel, and machinery. And, they depend on natural gas and petroleum imports for energy.

Today, manufacturing is a main part of the republic's economy. About 40 percent of Czechs work in this field. They produce iron, steel, glass, **textiles**, footwear, machinery, chemicals, and motor vehicles.

Another large employer is the service industry. It has been growing since the end of communism. Many people work in **real estate**, retail, and medical professions. Hotels and travel agencies have grown with increased tourism to the republic.

Agriculture is a small part of the Czech Republic's **economy**. Farmers mainly raise cattle, poultry, sheep, and pigs. The country's main crops are corn, oats, barley, rye, sugar beets, potatoes, and hops. Fishing brings in some money, too.

Tourism is important to Czechs. People from all over the world spend money while visiting the Czech Republic.

Historic Sites

Founded in the 800s, Prague is the Czech Republic's capital and largest city. This city lies on both sides of the Vltava River. Today, Prague is known for its amazing **architecture**, including Charles Bridge, Prague Castle, St. Vitus' Cathedral, and the Old Town buildings. And, it is one of the most beautiful cities in Europe.

Prague is a **cultural** center for Europe. But, it is also a center for trade. Machinery, tools, chemicals, metals, **textiles**, beer, and leather are all manufactured there.

Architect Frank Gehry's unusual Rasin Building in Prague looks like two people dancing. So, it has been nicknamed the Fred and Ginger Building after famous dancers Fred Astaire and Ginger Rogers.

Historic Sites

St. Vitus' Cathedral is located in the Prague Castle complex. Because of its many churches, Prague is known as the "City of a Hundred Spires."

The Czech Republic's Supreme Court is located in the country's second-largest city, Brno (BUHR-naw). It lies on the Svitava and Svratka rivers in southeastern Moravia. Many historic buildings are located in Brno's older section. In contrast, the rest of the city has many modern buildings.

Ostrava, the country's third-largest city, sits on the Oder and Ostravice rivers. Ostrava is the heart of the republic's industrial area. The region is known for its iron and steel factories. The people mine coal and produce chemicals, food, furniture, clothing, and building materials.

Travel and News

Trains are a fun, easy way to travel around the Czech Republic.

The Czech Republic's transportation system is well developed. About 5,900 miles (9,500 km) of railroad tracks connect the Czech Republic to neighboring countries. And in Prague, people have the option of riding the **subway**.

The republic also has more than 79,000 miles (127,000 km) of roads. A superhighway connects Prague, Brno, and Bratislava in Slovakia.

Air and sea travel are other transportation options. There are airports in Prague, Ostrava, and Plzeň (PUHL-zehn). The Elbe and Vltava rivers are main shipping routes. And, Prague and Děčín (DYEH-cheen) are chief ports. The Oder River links to the Baltic Sea and Szczecin (SHCHEHT-sheen), a port in Poland.

Under **communist** rule, the government controlled and approved publishers and communications companies. The government also owned the country's telephone, television, and radio systems.

Today, Czechs enjoy freedom of speech and the press. Radio and television stations are owned both privately and by the government. Czechs can watch local as well as foreign news. About 30 daily newspapers and 1,800 magazines, other newspapers, and journals are available. And, about 5 million people regularly surf the Internet.

Today, newspapers and magazines from around the globe are available in the Czech Republic.

Parliament Rules

Today, the Czech Republic is a **parliamentary democracy**. The **parliament** runs the legislature. Parliament consists of an 81-member Senate and a 200-member Chamber of Deputies. Chamber members serve four-year terms, while senators hold office for six years.

The parliament creates the country's laws. It also elects a president to serve a five-year term. The president is the head of state. He or she appoints judges and chooses the prime minister. The president also has the power to dissolve the Chamber.

The prime minister oversees the daily running of the government. He or she also appoints members to a cabinet. Together, they perform the executive work of the government.

The judicial branch consists of district, regional, and chief courts. Above them are the Supreme Administrative Court and the Constitutional Court. Most judges serve unlimited terms. However, Constitutional Court judges serve for ten years.

Parliament Rules **31**

For local government, the country is divided into 14 regions. An elected assembly governs each region. Smaller local governments run the cities, the towns, and the villages.

Prague Castle is the official residence of the Czech president.

Let's Celebrate!

Czechs proudly celebrate national holidays throughout the year. Restoration of Czech Independence Day observes when the Czech Republic was created from Czechoslovakia in 1993. This is remembered on January 1.

Other public holidays include Labor Day on May 1. May 8 is Liberation Day. This holiday remembers the end of fighting in Europe during **World War II**.

Statehood Day is on September 28. This is also Saint Wenceslas Day. This holiday honors the **patron saint** of the Czech Republic. October 28 is Czech Founding Day. On this day in 1918, independent Czechoslovakia was first formed.

Student protests in 1940, 1969, and 1989 led to changes in the Czech government. Czechs remember the actions taken by the students with Struggle for Freedom and **Democracy** Day on November 17.

Eggs are a sign that Easter is just around the corner. Traditionally, girls decorate eggs to give to boys on Easter Monday.

Let's Celebrate!

Religious holidays are important to many Czechs as well. Christian Czechs celebrate Easter as well as Christmas. Some holidays honor saints and other religious figures. July 5 celebrates Saints Cyril and Methodius, who brought Christianity to Moravia in 863. July 6 remembers religious reformer Jan Hus.

December 24 is the most festive day of the Christmas holiday. Czechs decorate Christmas trees. And, baby Jesus delivers presents!

Rich Culture

Czechs enjoy a variety of outdoor activities. Many people garden, hike, ski, or ice-skate. Soccer is popular in the Czech Republic, just as it is throughout Europe. Often, people gather in pubs to visit and play games. Czechs enjoy watching films and television, too.

Czech **culture** is strongly linked to the Czech language. Some of the first major writings date back to the 1300s. After that time, **satires**, romances, legends of saints, and religious works emerged in this language.

In the 1900s, some of the best Czech authors included Jaroslav Hašek and Karel Čapek. Čapek is credited with inventing the word "robot" for his 1920 play titled *R.U.R: Rossum's Universal Robots*. Author Franz Kafka was born in Prague but wrote in German. Most of his works were published after his death in 1924.

Czechs love sports! Their top-notch professional athletes have gained enthusiastic fans in a variety of sports.

After **World War II**, many authors criticized the **communist** government. As a result, some of them, such as Milan Kundera and Josef Škvorecký, were forced to leave the country. However since 1989, the government no longer controls the publishing industry.

Symphonies and operas are a traditional part of Czech **culture**. Today, people continue to appreciate pieces by 1800s musician Bedřich Smetana. Smetana was both an accomplished composer and the founder of the Czech national school of music. Czechs also enjoy jazz, folk, and rock music.

In crafting, Czechs are best known for making toys, traditional Bohemian jewelry, and glass ornaments. Artist René Roubíček is known for his glass designs and sculptures.

Traditional handmade puppets are sold throughout the Czech Republic.

Graphic arts are strong in Czech culture, too. For example, late-1800s artist Alphonse Mucha is famous for his **art nouveau** paintings. And, artist Josef Čapek drew a series of comic drawings during Adolf Hitler's rise to power. The series is titled *The Dictator's Boots*. Also known is Josef Lada, who drew the illustrations for Jaroslav Hašek's writings.

The Prague National Theatre is important to Czech history. Through art and drama, it has helped preserve Czech language, music, and culture.

The Czech Republic's libraries and museums house much of its people's work. The largest library is the National Library, located in Prague. Prague is also home to several museums. The National Museum and the National Gallery are located there. Prague's Museum of Decorative Arts showcases one of the world's largest glass collections.

The Czech Republic is bursting with history. Whether visitors prefer activity or education, there is something for everyone in this small but exciting country!

Glossary

architecture - the art of planning and designing buildings.
art nouveau - an elaborate style of decoration featuring flowing lines. Art nouveau flourished from the 1890s to 1910.
communism - a social and economic system in which everything is owned by the government and given to the people as needed. A person who believes in communism is called a communist.
culture - the customs, arts, and tools of a nation or people at a certain time.
democracy - a governmental system in which the people vote on how to run their country.
dialect - a form of a language spoken in a certain area or by certain people.
dictator - a ruler with complete control who usually governs in a cruel or unfair way.
economy - the way a nation uses its money, goods, and natural resources.
European Union - an organization of European countries that works toward political, economic, governmental, and social unity.
free market - an economy that is not controlled by the government.
Germanic - of people of northwestern Europe in the Middle Ages.
NATO - North Atlantic Treaty Organization. A group formed by the United States, Canada, and some European countries in 1949. It tries to create peace among its nations and protect them from common enemies.
parliament - the highest lawmaking body of some governments.

parliamentary democracy - a form of government in which the decisions of the nation are made by the people through the elected parliament.
patron saint - a saint believed to be the special protector of a church, a city, a state, or a country.
plateau - a raised area of flat land.
Protestant - a Christian who does not belong to the Catholic Church.
real estate - property, which includes buildings and land.
rebellion - an armed resistance or defiance of a government. To rebel is to disobey an authority or the government.
satire - writing that makes fun of human faults.
subway - an electric railroad that runs beneath city streets.
textile - a woven fabric or cloth.
World War I - from 1914 to 1918, fought in Europe. Great Britain, France, Russia, the United States, and their allies were on one side. Germany, Austria-Hungary, and their allies were on the other side.
World War II - from 1939 to 1945, fought in Europe, Asia, and Africa. Great Britain, France, the United States, the Soviet Union, and their allies were on one side. Germany, Italy, Japan, and their allies were on the other side.

Web Sites

To learn more about the Czech Republic, visit ABDO Publishing Company on the World Wide Web at **www.abdopublishing.com**. Web sites about the Czech Republic are featured on our Book Links page. These links are routinely monitored and updated to provide the most current information available.

Index

A
animals 18, 19, 25
architecture 26, 27
arts 8, 34, 36, 37
Austria 10, 14, 24

B
Baltic Sea 28

C
Charles IV (king) 9
cities 4, 9, 20, 22, 26, 27, 28, 31, 34, 37
climate 16
communication 29
Czechoslovakia 4, 5, 8, 10, 11, 12, 13, 20, 32

D
Danube River 16

E
economy 12, 13, 20, 24, 25, 26, 27
education 22
Elbe River 16, 28
European Union 13

F
food 22, 25, 27

G
Germany 8, 10, 11, 12, 14, 16, 20, 24

government 10, 12, 13, 19, 20, 22, 24, 27, 29, 30, 31, 32, 35

H
Habsburgs 10
Hitler, Adolf 10, 36
holidays 22, 32, 33
housing 20
Hungary 8, 20, 24
Hus, Jan 9, 33

J
Jizera River 16

L
land 4, 14, 16, 18, 19
language 10, 20, 22, 34
literature 34, 35, 36, 37

M
Masaryk, Tomáš 10
Morava River 16
Munich Agreement 11
music 36

N
NATO 13
natural resources 14, 16, 24, 27

O
Oder River 16, 27, 28
Ohře River 16

Ostravice River 27

P
plants 18
Poland 8, 14, 16, 20, 28

R
regions 4, 8, 9, 10, 11, 14, 16, 20, 27, 33
religion 9, 10, 22, 33, 34
Russia 24

S
Slovakia 4, 5, 8, 13, 14, 16, 20, 24, 28
sports 34
Svitava River 27
Svratka River 27

T
Thirty Years' War 10
transportation 28

V
Velvet Revolution 13
Vltava River 16, 26, 28

W
World War I 10
World War II 11, 12, 20, 32, 35